MW01009554

The Fox Judge and Other Tales

The Fox Judge and Other Tales

Translated and Retold by
Maria Zemko Tetro and Joseph A. Tetro

Illustrations by
Olesya Sikora and Dzvinka Zagajska

Published by
Winter Light Books, Inc.
Garden City, New York

Library of Congress Control Number: 2007940120

Published in the United States of America

Tetro, Maria Zemko.
The fox judge and other tales / translated and retold by Maria Zemko Tetro and Joseph A. Tetro ; illustrations by Olesya Sikora and Dzvinka Zagajska.
p. cm.
SUMMARY: Three Ukrainian folk tales depict a special hen that lays a golden egg, a sly fox who negotiates an argument between two cats trying to divide a wedge of cheese, and three butterflies of different colors who stay together to help each other through a sudden rainstorm.
Audience: Grades 2-3.
LCCN 2007940120
ISBN-13: 978-09797372-1-3
ISBN-10: 0-9797372-1-4

1. Tales--Ukraine. [1. Folklore--Ukraine.]
I. Tetro, Joseph A. II. Sikora, Olesya, ill.
III. Zagajska, Dzvinka, ill. IV. Title.

PZ8.1.F69 2007 398.2'09477
QBI07-600315

for Pasha and Yurko

The Spotted Hen

Once there was a Grandma and Grandpa
Who had a spotted hen.
One day the hen layed an egg,
Not a simple one,
But a golden one.

Grandma tried and Grandpa too
To break the egg for food,
But they could not make a dent
Until a mouse running by,
Twisted his tail high

And broke the egg in two.
Grandma cried and Grandpa too
Because there was
No more food for them,
But said the spotted hen,

Don't cry, Grandma,
Don't cry, Grandpa,
I will lay another egg,
Not a golden one,
But a simple one.

The Fox Judge

Once there were two cats that lived happily in a country village. One day they found a wedge of cheese and talked about how they could share it. Both cats wanted an equal part, but they could not decide how to divide it.

One cat said,

> *"Let's cut it across"*

The second cat said,

> *"No, it's better to do it length-wise."*

And so they argued, back and forth.

While the cats were trying to decide, a fox walked by. She saw the piece of cheese, and the cats, then asked them:

"What is going on? Why are you arguing?"

"Well," said the cats, *"We don't know how to divide this lump of cheese."*

"Oh," said the fox, *"That can be done easily." "Let me divide it for you."*

The cats gave her the cheese, and she broke it into two halves.

"No, this piece is larger. Let's even it out."

And she took a bite from the larger piece.

"Now, this one is bigger. I'll trim just a bit more so each of you gets the same size."

The cats looked at each other, and at the fox, but she said,

"I must be just and be sure each of you has an equal share."

Then, she took another bite.

Each time the fox was trying to make the cuts even, she took another bite. From one side and the other, the fox kept eating until there were only two very small pieces left.

"Well," said the fox, *"Here you have two even pieces. You can weigh them on a scale if you like, but they are perfect."*

"That is all very well," said the cats, *"but you ate most of our cheese." "Why did you take so much?"*

"Why?" asked the fox. *"Didn't I divide it fairly for you?"*

Come out, Mr. Sun, come out,
Over grandfather's fields
And grandmother's herbs,

In our yard and
Over the spring flowers,

On the children
As they are playing,
Waiting for you.

— *from a collection of Ukrainian poems*

Three Butterflies

Once there were three small butterflies flying in a large garden. Each butterfly was different: one was white, the second, red, and the third, yellow.

All day long the sun was shining, and they flew happily from flower to flower. To each one they whispered something, took a little nectar, and flew away.

As the butterflies played, no one noticed that the clouds were covering the sun.

Soon, it started to rain.

The butterflies began to feel the water on their wings. They hurried around the garden, looking for a dry place, but they could not find one anywhere.

The butterflies didn't know what to do. They were getting soaked in the rain, barely able to move their little wings.

At the other end of the garden, the butterflies saw a few flowers large enough to keep them dry.

They flew through the rain, wings fluttering up and down. Finally, they reached a tulip, a bright red and yellow one.

"Dear tulip," they said, *"Please hide us from the rain."*

The tulip looked at them,

"Yellow and red butterflies I will hide,
but the white one must stay outside."

But the red and yellow butterflies protested,

"If you won't protect our brother,
we would rather be wet."

So the butterflies flew away to a white lily nearby.

They asked her to help hide them from the rain. She, too, looked at all the butterflies, but said she could only take the white one.

> *"I won't hide by myself,"* the white butterfly said, *"We must be safe together."*

With that, they flew away again.

All the time the sun was listening behind the clouds.

He wanted to see those friends that stayed together. Forcing his way through the clouds, he sent bright sunlight to the butterflies.

Their wings dry again, the butterflies felt warm and happy, dancing in the garden until sunset, when they went home to sleep.

©2007

About the Artists

Olesya Sikora and Dzvinka Zagajska

Born in Ukraine and a graduate of the Lviv Academy of Art, Olesya has taught at the Little Academy of Art in Pidbuz and is currently a teacher at The Children's Art School in Drohobych.

With her daughter, Dzvinka, a student at the Lviv Academy of Art and a member of *Plast*, the Ukrainian scouts organization, Olesya has collaborated on several projects, including books from *KOLO*, the children's book publishing company.

This is the first time these artists have been published in the United States.

Acknowledgments

In helping us research archival sources, the assistance of the librarians and aides at the Shevchenko Scientific Society of New York and the Ukrainian Institute of America is gratefully acknowledged.

We also wish to recognize the contribution from the staff at the Palace of Art in Drohobych, Ukraine, whose knowledge of, and work with, local artists was invaluable to us.

Although it requires no formal expression, we mention the encouragement of friends and family and are honored to repay their advocacy by this publication.

Finally, we owe much to the folk tales themselves, Ukrainian in origin but perhaps universal in theme, beautifully drawn by Olesya and Dzvinka, and hope they will speak to you and your young readers.

— *from the Publishers*